T0310058

The Book of One Hundred Riddles of the Fairy Bellaria

The Book of One Hundred Riddles of the Fairy Bellaria

by

Charles Godfrey Leland

Edited and with an Introduction by

Jack Zipes

Distributed by the
University of Minnesota Press
Minneapolis
London

New material copyright 2018 by Jack Zipes

Published by Little Mole and Honey Bear, LTD, Minneapolis, MN

First published by T. Fisher Unwin, London, 1892

Layout by Martin Skoro and Ross Rezac, MartinRoss Design

Printed by Anderberg Innovative Print Solutions

Distributed by the University of Minnesota Press
111 Third Avenue South, Suite 290
Minneapolis, MN 55401-2520
http://www.upress.umn.edu

ISBN 978-1-5179-0608-5 (hc)

Printed in the United States of America on acid-free paper

The University of Minnesota is an equal-opportunity educator and employer.

Dedicated to my good friends

Martin Skoro
and
Ross Rezac

Charles Godfrey Leland: An American Phenomenon

Jack Zipes

As a folklorist, he was condescendingly tolerated by the academic community, even in his own day. Said one of them, "Leland could do very well as a folklorist, but he had too many irons in the fire." . . . His crime was a passionate interest in all life around him, and his own life was full of many activities. His transgressions were that he was a successful popular writer—his books sold in large numbers— and that his interests lay in many fields of literary endeavor. The truly great and cultured men of the day—Holmes, Emerson, Washington Irving, Poe and many others—recognized Leland's true value. Now and then, through the years, a voice arose in just defense and in recognition of Leland's great literary talent, but, unfortunately, such expressions came only on rare occasions.

—Moritz Jagendorf, *New York Folklore Quarterly*

In a memorial written by the British folklorist, F. York Powell, the year Charles Godfrey Leland (1824-1903) died, Powell described him as follows: "American born but living and dying in Europe, a graduate of Princeton, a student of Heidelberg, of Munich, and of Paris, a barrister, an educationalist, a traveler, a volunteer soldier both in the States and in Europe, a skilled handicraftsman, a fair designer, and an excellent companion, Charles Godfrey Leland would have been a man of mark even had he not been also one of the first humorous poets of his time and country, and a devoted explorer in the enchanted fields of linguistic and folklore." (*Folk-Lore*, 14, 1903).

Of course, Powell's description of this phenomenal man needs a bit more explanation if we are to grasp how truly exceptional Leland was. Born into a wealthy and privileged family in Philadelphia, he was a curious boy who showed a clear interest in the supernatural and occult literature during his youth. Legend has it that, soon after his birth, an old Dutch nurse carried him up to the garret of the house and performed a strange ritual. She placed a Bible, a key, and a knife on his breast. Then she added lighted candles, money, and a plate of salt at his head. This ritual was to guarantee that Leland would be fortunate in his life and eventually become a scholar and a wizard. Whether this incident ever occurred, we do know that his interest in fairy tales, folklore, witchcraft, and the supernatural was fostered by different household servants (Irish and African American), who told him marvelous tales. Moreover, by the time he turned six, he had already become a voracious reader of occult literature.

However, Leland was not a particularly good student in the private and public schools he attended, showing more interest in the occult than in the pedagogical curriculum. Nevertheless, in 1842, he was accepted as a student by Princeton University, and his father hoped that he would turn his attention to the serious study of jurisprudence. Instead, Leland spent most of his time learning classical and foreign languages, reading philosophy and occult literature, and avoiding science and mathematics classes. Moreover, he formed very few friendships and disliked the atmosphere at Princeton very much. In fact, he took a greater interest in extra-curricular activities and the arts than the rigid Princeton curriculum. The result was that he graduated last in his class in 1845. Yet, despite his father's disappointment, he gave his son an allowance to study and educate himself for three years in Europe. This was common practice among rich American families: Europe was considered a finishing school where young Americans were to learn proper manners, etiquette, and civility, not to mention how to form connections with notable Europeans.

In Leland's case—he was only twenty-two at the time—he explored all types of fields especially linguistics and philosophy in Heidelberg and Munich, traveled to Italy, France, and the Netherlands, learned to speak German and French fluently, and also spent a good deal of time in taverns breaking free of puritanical inhibitions. Early in 1848, toward the end of his European education, he went to Paris to study at the Sorbonne and soon took the side of the republicans during the revolution, often fighting on the barricades for the liberty of the French people. Though his life was often in danger, he managed to survive the conflicts in the city and returned to Philadelphia that same year to begin a study of law.

His father was pleased by his son's choice, but Leland never practiced law even though he passed the Pennsylvanian bar exams in 1851. Instead, he began devoting himself to journalism and worked at first for *The Knickerbocker*, a magazine in New York. A gifted writer and dilettante, Leland could and did write on any topic—social and political articles, culture, theater, and music reviews. He also published a humorous book called *Meister Karl's Sketch-Book* (1955) and translated Heinrich Heine's poetry. During the next fifteen years, he was an editor for *The Illustrated News*, *The Evening Bulletin*, and *Graham's Magazine* and continued to publish humorous articles. During this time he became engaged to and married Eliza Isabel Fisher in 1856, the daughter of a prominent Philadelphia family, who remained wedded to the peripatetic Leland her entire life. This in itself was a remarkable achievement, for it was difficult to keep up with Leland. A tall man, over six-feet, he was exceedingly charming if not charismatic. Articulate, curious, and filled with different projects, he was searching at that time for a career and life style that would set his multiple creative talents free. Most of all, he did not want steady employment. A liberal thinker, who detested slavery, Leland enlisted in the Union Army in 1863 and fought at the Battle of Gettysburg. At the end of the Civil War, he returned to Philadelphia to become the managing editor of *The Philadelphia Press* in 1865.

Then, in November of 1867, Leland's father died and left him a considerable inheritance that would allow him to live the life he desired until his death. It was a life of the Other, so to speak. In fact, it had been clear ever since his first sojourn in Europe that Leland did not want to be a Philadelphian or even an American, nor did he necessarily want to be defined as an ex-patriot or European. Leland was simply fascinated by the cultures of other people such as the gypsies in England, the Indians in America, the Italians in northern Italy, and witches and witchcraft in Europe. In short, the money he inherited from his father allowed him to become the Other, who felt impelled to discover and preserve the customs and values of marginal groups before they disappeared.

Consequently, in 1869, Leland and his wife left Philadelphia for London, which they made their home base until 1879. Actually, he arrived in London as an American celebrity, for his book, *Hans Breitmann's Ballads* was published in 1869 and made him famous as one of the foremost American humorists. This highly unusual book contained numerous anecdotes told in a strange German-American dialect by Meister Karl about the comic adventures of a fictitious German named Hans Breitmann, who bumbled his way through life. It became a huge success in America and England

and remained popular through the nineteenth and twentieth centuries. Indeed, the period from 1869 to 1879 was significant for Leland, who became more of a folklorist and began identifying with the English Romany. At a certain point, the gypsies began ito call him "the Rye," a respectable gentleman, a name he adopted, and accepted him in their society, while he studied their customs and published four books about them: *The English Gypsies* (1873), *English Gypsy Songs* (1875) in collaboration with E. H. Palmer and Janet Tuckey, *The Gypsies* (1882), and *Gypsy Sorcery and Fortune-Telling* (1891). In addition to these studies, Leland traveled on the Continent to do more research on differences among the European gypsies.

In 1879, Leland and his wife returned to Philadelphia, where he shifted gears so to speak and began work on two very different projects: the introduction of the minor arts into public schools and the study of the Algonquin Indians in nearby New Brunswick. Leland, who had always been a talented amateur artist and had a strong interest in the decorative arts, developed a program in the so-called minor arts to help children who did not want to go to college. With the help of many educators, he founded The Industrial Art School in 1881 and taught there without pay for three years.

In addition, he frequently visited the Passamaquoddy Indians in New Brunswick, learned their language, and eventually published *The Algonquin Legends* (1884), which included commentaries about the lore of Native Americans.

To say the least, the four years in Philadelphia were highly productive as Leland, once again, tried to become at one with the Other—this time with native Americans, and he was also made an honorary member of one of the western tribes. However, Leland and his wife longed for Europe, and they returned to London in 1884, stayed there briefly, and eventually settled in Florence for the rest of their lives. Now Leland's passion for recovering the remnants of ancient lore and tales turned to Italy. In 1886, he had met an extraordinary woman named Maddalena, who was a witch/fortune teller. Over the next fifteen years she was one of his major sources for three different books, *Etruscan-Roman Remains in Popular Tradition* (1893), *Legends of Florence* (1895-96), and *Aradia, or The Gospel of the Witches* (1899). While these three books have different subject matter, they all share Leland's historical quest to recover the ancient origins of rituals and customs that formed the basis of stories and incantations disseminated among the common people in northern Italy. His aim was to prove that superstition and magic were related to deeply held beliefs of the Italians and were not to be dismissed as trivial. Moreover, it is apparent in all these works that he had a deep respect for women and their rights, and that they played a significant role as witches and fairies in his effort to comprehend the essence of Italian folklore.

It was also during this period that Leland took some of his spare time, if he really had any, to write and design *The Book of One Hundred Riddles of the Fairy Bellaria* (1892), which has never been adequately studied nor republished since its original publication in London by T. Fisher Unwin. This is a most unusual book, surprisingly neglected by Leland scholars. In my opinion, it is exceptional because it brings together elements of his research on Etruscan myths, his strong belief in the power and intelligence of women expressed in his eccentric study, *The Alternate Sex or The Female Intellect in Man, and The Masculine in Woman* (1904), and his amateur work as designer of images that emanated from his pioneer work in the arts and crafts movement in England and Philadelphia.

Leland's heroine in *Bellaria* bears some resemblance to Scheherazade in *The One Thousand and One Nights*, which he certainly knew. However, Bellaria is more powerful and mysterious. She is not just a clever and courageous fairy but an obscure Etruscan goddess, often called Alpan or Alpena. She was the goddess of spring, flowers, love, fate, and death. In Tuscan folklore, Alpena is generally called Bellaria, a sylph or winged fairy linked to springtime, flowers, and love. In another of Leland's neglected works, *Unpublished Legends of Virgil* (1899), he remarks: "It is said that Bellaria is the sister of Mercury, and that both fly in the air. When the *fate* or fairies, or good witches die, Bellaria descends, and then bears their souls to heaven."

In many respects, Leland constantly paid homage to the acute intelligence of women in *Bellaria* and in his folklore research. After his arrival in Florence some time in 1885, he began working closely with the practicing witch, Maddalena, who provided him with an immense amount of information about Italian folklore, witchcraft, customs, and beliefs. Undoubtedly, she played a role in suggesting Bellaria as the fairy goddess who can outwit a tyrant. Finally, it is also important to know that Leland's wife, Eliza Isabel Fisher, was generally referred to as "Bella" by relatives and friends due to her beauty and intelligence. Clearly, Leland had many reasons for naming his brave and intelligent fairy Bellaria.

Yet, why, during the last decade of his life, did Leland choose to create this small book that made a strong statement against injustice and barbarous kings? Why does Bellaria, who punishes the cruel king for his oppression and cruel wars, vanish at the end of Leland's tale? We can never be certain exactly why Leland made these choices and decided to produce this unusual book which he personally designed, illustrated, and wrote, but it is clear that he was somewhat influenced by the rise of the suffragette movement in England and America as well as the great resurgence of interest in fairies and stories featuring strong heroines in fairy tales and fantasy literature. Such writers as George MacDonald, Lewis Carroll, Maria Louisa Molesworth, Laurence Houseman, Edith Nesbit, and many other British writers (not to mention L. Frank Baum in America) were publishing stories and novels featuring talented female protagonists who struggle to rectify the injustices in their societies. Not only were the 1880s and 1890s the golden age of fairy tales, but also folklorists like Joseph Jacobs and Andrew Lang contributed to the fairy-tale renaissance, and Leland was fully aware of the sociocultural developments in Great Britain. It was through the other worlds of the fairy tale that writers were seeking justice, and through Bellaria, Leland, too, sought to pass on a message of courage to future generations in his own unique way. Simply put, he was a phenomenon who lived to serve the cause of Otherness.

Note on the Text

This reproduction of Leland's *Bellaria* is based on the first and only edition of the book, published in England by T. Fisher Unwin. All the illustrations were drawn by Leland himself. He was an unusually gifted amateur artist. I have edited his quaint "Shakespearean" language a great deal, and I hope that I have not diminished his unique style and intention. Leland loved the power of imagination.

THE HUNDRED RIDDLES
of
THE FAIRY BELLARIA

Once there was a fairy who was very wise and knew all things. She fell in love with a king and would eventually marry him. This king had a wonderful garden, full of all kinds of fruit, and if any one entered it without permission, that person would be beheaded. One morning the fairy, whose name was Bellaria, entered the garden and began to eat the fruit. There the King caught her, and, thinking she was just a normal woman, said that she must die, unless she answered an unusual question.

"Call your council," she said, "and ask your question before your council so that I may be fairly judged."

So he called together all his wise men and asked: "How many hairs do I have on my head?"

And she answered, "Just so many as I have on mine, which is thirty thousand, lacking one. And if you doubt it, pull out a hair, and I will pull out one of mine, and so on till all are gone."

But the King would not do this, and a very wise man who was present said:

"Oh, King, the maiden is not far from the truth, for it is said that in a full head there are thirty thousand hairs."

So the King, seeing that the maiden was wise, married her, but said to her:

"When I was born, a very wise witch declared that I would be lucky in life, except in one thing, which was that a time would come when I would lose what I loved most, yet keep what I liked best, or what was best for me and mine, or for my people."

Then the Queen replied, "I will answer this in due time, but things would not go good for you if I answered it now."

So, they lived together happily for many years and had a son who was as beautiful as the sun, moon, and stars, and his hair was like falling water.

Now, there was another king—a cruel, evil man—who was far more powerful than this one, and he came with a great army and took his kingdom from him. But, loving wisdom and cleverness above all things, and having once sworn an oath that he would never harm anyone who could outwit him, this cruel king decided to test the Queen after hearing that she was so extraordinarily clever. Consequently, one day he told her that if she could answer the hundred riddles which he would pose to her, he would never harm her husband and would depart in peace. However, if she could not answer them, she and her husband would die.

"Life for life," she answered. "Yours against mine. This will be the only way I answer your riddles!"

Then the King became angry. Yet, since he was certain that no one living could guess his riddles, he consented. Therefore, a great meeting was held, and all the wise men present were to remember what was said.

Once the riddling started, the King, whose name was Ruggero, said: "Off with your head, oh Queen, unless you answer me this riddle: What have you often seen fall, but never rise?"

The Queen's response was short and sweet:

> *The snow which falls upon the plain*
> *will never rise as snow again.*

Then King Ruggero said, "Off with your head, oh Queen, unless you answer me this riddle: In my palace there is a lady who is extremely beautiful, who was never born, and who will never die. She has eyes, but sees not; ears, yet hears

not; a nose, but smells not; and hands as well shaped as yours, yet feels not."

To this the Queen sang with her harp:

You have at home against the wall,
a marble statue in your hall,
which is your dwelling's chief adorn,
yet never indeed of woman born.
She has no death to fear, and why?
What never lived can never die.

Then there was a cry of admiration in the hall, and King Ruggero cast up his head approvingly, and said "Truly, I have no fool to deal with in you! But off with your head, oh Queen, unless you answer me this: Who is she who puts on all her clothes when it is hot and goes naked when it freezes?"

Then the Queen sang with her harp:

The apple tree in summer time,
When it is hot, is in her prime.
A garment green is what she wears.
And many verdant leafs she bears.
But when the winter chills the land,
Then she is naked as my hand.
And to you, oh King, I must confess
Such riddles are not hard to guess.

Then King Ruggero bit his lip and said, "Off with your head, oh Queen, unless you answer me this: Who is he far beneath you, and often under your very feet, yet who pays you no respect, and heeds you not, nor respects your rule?"

Then the Queen laughed and sang with her harp:

Beneath my feet in mud or clay,
Mole or earthworm makes his way,
Little heed he gives, I've seen,
To any king or any queen,
And cares no more our likes to please
Than I for riddles light as these.

King Ruggero replied, "Praise the day when the sun sets, and not before. But off with your head, oh Queen, unless you can answer me this: What is it that grows colder the more it burns?"

Then the Queen sang:

Take a taper from your room
Out into the frost and gloom,
Yet while burning, as we know,
It must ever colder grow.

I grow cooler, on my word,
While you grow hot with fear, my lord!

"There is a long furrow yet to plough," answered Ruggero.
"Off with your head, oh Queen, unless you answer me this:

What is ever running away and afar, yet which never departs from one place?"

Then the Queen sang:

> *A river runs through rocks and plains,*
> *Yet ever in its bed remains,*
> *Even as your riddles run;*
> *While I am here as I begun,*
> *As our life cloth come and go,*
> *So the waters onward flow.*

King Ruggero replied, "That is well said, my Queen, but off with your head if you cannot answer me this: What is that which sees everything save itself?"

And the Queen sang:

> *My eyes I never yet did see,*
> *Yet they behold all things for me.*
> *Your mind sees all beneath your control,*
> *Yet you never saw your soul.*
> *With double riddle you would cheat,*
> *With double answer you are beat.*

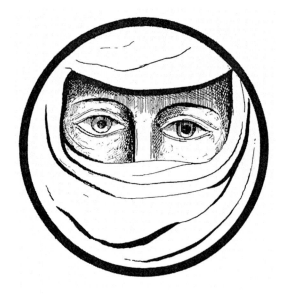

King Ruggero answered, "Never was woman born who was as crafty as you. But to a hard knot of wood, a sharp axe. Answer me this, oh Queen, or off with your head! What is it tells our secrets, yet never knows them?"

The Queen sang:

The ink with which we secrets write
Nothing knows what we indict.
And the pen from which it flows,
Of it all as little knows.

The King said, "Answer me this, oh Queen, or off with

your head! What is the bird with an iron bill, which never flies until you pull its tail?"

The Queen sang:

> *The arrow has the sharpest bill,*
> *With feathers stripped from many a quill;*
> *Naught to fly does it avail,*

Until we pull it by the tail.
King, your shafts are all in vain,
And your shooting gives you pain.

Ruggero replied, "My quiver is not as yet empty. So, off with your head, oh Queen, or answer me this: Where is the Red Sea in which men live but never drown?"

The Queen sang:

> *Blood is the sea in which we live,*
> *Which unto us our life does give.*
> *It has its ebb, it has its flow.*
> *It has its tide as all men know;*
> *But when the motion ceases,*
> *death comes unto man and stops his breath.*
> *As all thy waves of riddles, friend,*
> *Bring you still nearer to your end.*

The king frowned and said, "Off with your head, Oh Queen, unless you can answer me this: What gave death while it was alive, and now gives life now that it is dead?"

The queen sang:

> *While he was alive the horn*
> *By a savage bull was worn.*
> *Now the horn, though it be dead,*
> *Filled with ale, or wine, or mead,*
> *When we pass it, round about*
> *Gives life to all who drink it out.*

In response, the King said, "Off with your head, oh Queen, unless you can answer me this: Who was the traveler who was pursued by a murderer and left a forest behind him?"

The Queen sang:

A bird shot through the air and still
Carried an acorn in his bill.
Pursuing the bird a falcon flew;
he let the acorn drop. Unto
The ground it fell, and there it grew.

So from it others came, and there
Arose in time a forest fair.
You drop acorn-riddles, King,
From which in time great woe will spring.

"That woe will be to you," said Ruggero. "Off with your head, oh Queen, unless you can answer me this: Who is it that never lives till he is hanged, and who dies when he is cut down?"

The Queen sang:

The apple on a tree was born,
And there it hangs from night to morn.
And there it swings from morn to night,
All through the summer, in delight,
Till it is plucked in autumn, when
It is devoured by beasts or men,
And as it falls from the tree,
You, my King, will no longer be.

Then Ruggero turned red and white with pride and anger, and said, "Look to it that you, too, do not swing on a tree and are not thrown to wild beasts to be devoured. Off with

your head, oh Queen, unless you can answer me this: What is that creature which is one while it flies, and many when it falls. Many it kills, and many it serves in many ways when it becomes one again?"

The Queen sang:

> *The cloud which flies before the sun*
> *While it is in the air is one,*
> *Falling in raindrops to the ground.*

> *Then it is, changed to many, found,*
> *And by it many a man is drowned,*
> *While many others over it row,*
> *And drink the water as they go.*
> *Thus may this stream of riddles, too,*
> *Fuel my life and be death to you!*

Then there was laughter from everyone in the hall, so merrily and boldly that the Queen twanged the harp, and stared daringly at the King. And he, looking grim and holding his beard in his hand, said, "Off with your head, oh Queen, unless you answer me this: What are the two colors which fight the most, one with another?"

The Queen sang:

> *White is the dead man as he lies,*
> *White is the earth when autumn dies.*
> *And high or low, or far or near,*
> *All things turn white with cold or fear.*
> *The fox or ermine in the snow*
> *From winter weather whiter grow.*
> *White bones and teeth, since he began,*

Were aye the deadest part of man.
And sailors say when water dies,
As snow-white foam it upwards flies,
But when the summer comes again,

She clothes with green the wood and plain.
Green is the grass and green the trees,
And green the wheat waves in the breeze.
With white, the green has ever strife,
For life is green and green is life.
Your lips, oh King, are white I see,
And soon they will even whiter be;
For while this game is sport to me,
You'll soon be dead and never free.

Then Ruggero replied, "Off with your head, my Queen, unless you can answer me this: Where are the birds which never flew, the flowers which never took root, men who never moved, women who never loved and never told a secret; where are all things that ever lived on earth with all their colors fresh and fair, yet all dead. What do you call the place wherein all this is found?"

The Queen sang:

Birds in a picture never flew,
Buds that were painted never blew;
Men who were drawn by human hand,

Did never live in any land;
Maids of their kind no one could move,
They never hear a word of love.
For these and everything go look,
And you may find them in a book.

All dead and still you'll see them there,
Yet with their colors fresh and fair.

Ruggero replied, "Off with your head, oh Queen unless
you can answer me this: What animals truly make the

sweetest sounds? Answer me, or else you die!"

The Queen sang:

> *From the cat, and sheep, and bear,*
> *Cords are made which everywhere,*
> *Stretched upon the minstrel's harp,*
> *Utter music soft or sharp,*
> *Which they better and more sweetly sing*
> *Than the nightingale in spring.*
> *So the squalling cat, in faith,*
> *May sing full sweetly after death.*

Then the King responded, "Who are the five brothers who have only one hand among them, yet who do all things so well with it that they need no more?"

The Queen sang:

> *Fingers are the brothers five,*
> *Well they work, and hard they strive;*
> *In this world are none, I say,*
> *Who can do such work as they.*
> *And yet fall what may befall,*

There's but one hand among them all.

Ruggero said, "Off with your head, oh Queen, unless you can answer me this: What is the name of the bird

which never flies away nor soars on high till it is tied fast, and which when free no longer roams?"

The queen sang:

The kite in air can never glide
Until with a cord it's firmly tied.
Once that's done it will be more sure,
Unless it's bound, it cannot soar.
Even so, upon this earth we see,
Men who never think of liberty,
And never rise to thought because
They are not bound by faith or laws.
What makes our spirit soar at last
Is ever that which holds it fast."

Ruggero said, "Lady, you are, indeed, wise. But though the fox runs faster than man, he will eventually be caught by the man. So, off with your head, oh Queen, unless you can answer me this: Who is the best and bravest knight, the one of most worth, yet with no armor save his shirt, and that thin, and who are the worthless men, well clad and completely covered with the strongest mail?"

The Queen sang:

The sweetest fruit has a cover thin,
Nothing thicker than its skin.

The apple, who does take the prize,
The sun and rain and wind defies;
While pine-tree seeds, and nuts as well,
Are deeply cased in hardest shell.

Yet the time will come aright
When they, too, must see the light,
Like you, oh King, with all your strength
Will come to certain death at length.

52

The King said nothing, but drank a can of ale, and then cried, "Off with your head, oh Queen, unless you can answer me this: Who were the two who were put to bed to save their lives, and who ate their covering before they stood up?"

Then the Queen sang:

> *The caterpillar, as we know,*
> *To sleep in silken sheet cloth does go.*
> *Then as a butterfly so bright,*
> *She eats it through and comes to light.*
> *There was a king, the story goes,*
> *Who once, when fleeing from his foes,*
> *Was hidden, as if in a bed,*
> *Beneath a tile of winter bread.*
> *And while thus covered, head and limb,*
> *He ate the loaves, which sheltered him.*
> *King, you eat your loaves full steam ahead*
> *And this will cost you soon your head.*
> *For every riddle, every breath,*
> *Is one step nearer to your death.*

Full of anger, the King yelled, "Off with your head, oh
Queen, unless you can answer me this: Who is the politest
and best bred among arms or weapons?"

The Queen sang:

> *Of all the weapons that I know,*
> *The gentlest mannered is the bow,*

Because with grace it always tends
Before it afar an arrow sends,
And makes a bow as we may see
Before it attacks his enemy
As nobles do of high degree.

Then the King said, "Off with your head, oh Queen,

unless you can answer this question: Who are they who shine in deepest darkness, yet give no light?"

The Queen sang:

> *Gold and silver, copper, lead,*
> *Deeply buried in their earthly bed,*
> *Have their hidden glow, yet none*
> *Can shine until they see the sun.*
> *So it's true, and many know it,*
> *That frequently a brilliant poet*
> *Never shines till he can sing*
> *His verses to a mighty king.*

"By my life," cried Ruggero, "that was well said! But off with your head, oh Queen, unless you can answer me this: What is that white thing which is red while it is green, and fairest when it is black?"

The Queen sang:

> *In the bud a blackberry,*
> *Is white as snow, we all agree.*
> *Going onward from a flower,*

It is red while green and sour,
But when sweet and fair to see
It is black as black can be.

Ruggero said, "Off with your head, oh Queen, unless you can answer me this question : What was that which had four legs and ran over the land on two, yet which never stirred a foot?"

The Queen sang:

A *thief, who stole a lamb one day,*
Carried it on his back away.
Upon two feet he did rove,
And yet no limb the lamb did move.

"Off with your head, oh Queen," the King declared, unless you can answer this: What do all men most fear, yet most desire?"

And the Queen sang:

> To that question answers seven
> Might easily be given.
> Fleetly from your tongue they'd run.
> But I'll sum them all in one.
> What men seek in every hour,
> Most especially, it is power,
> And it's what they mostly fear,
> Be it far away in God, or just near.
> But of one thing certain be,
> Your power wakes no fear in me.

Ruggero replied, "We have all the time until sunrise, for the sun has just set. So, off with your head, oh Queen, unless you can answer me this: Who is the giant with two stone jaws who eats and swallows your food before you can even taste it?"

The Queen sang:

A mighty giant is the mill,
Who eats, yet never has his fill.
Between the high and lower stone
He chews up all that's to him thrown.
But if he did not chew the corn,

There'd be no bread for any born.

The King replied, "Off with your head, oh Queen, unless you can answer me this question: What does every man leave behind him in this world?"

The Queen sang:

Not their bodies, for it's known
Some saints alive to heaven have gone.
Nor is it their earthly fame,
For many never left a name.
But all save those of feet bereft,
Behind them have their footprints left.

King Ruggero replied: "Off with your head, oh Queen, unless you can answer me this: Who is it of this earth that when he pleases sits in judgment on the mightiest king?"

The Queen sang:

> *When the king in judgment sits,*
> *Though he uses all his wits,*
> *The fly who lands upon his hair,*
> *Sits on him in the judgment there.*

King Ruggero said, "Off with your head, oh Queen, unless you can answer me this: how would a dwarf give a riddle to a giant?"

The Queen sang:

> *As the dwarf is weak and small*
> *As the giant is strong and tall,*
> *Like a slip 'twixt lip and cup,*
> *Between them they must give it up.*

The King said, "Off with your head, oh Queen, unless you

can answer me this: What crosses the water, yet never gets across it?"

The Queen sang:

> *The bridge which goes from shore to shore*
> *Crosses the stream, yet never gets over it*

The King said, "Off with your head, my Queen, unless you can answer me this: "I once saw a bridge over which many passed, and then the bridge walked on after them."

The Queen sang:

Two men joined hands from shore to shore;
Their wives on them passed safely over.
One drew his friend to where he stood.
So all got past the roaring flood.
Two men joined hands from shore to shore;

Their wives on them passed safely over.
One drew his friend to where he stood.
So all got past the roaring flood.
Two men joined hands from shore to shore;
Their wives on them passed safely over.

> *One drew his friend to where he stood.*
> *So all got past the roaring flood.*

The King said, "Off with your head, oh Queen, unless you can answer me this: What things leave no mark behind them, yet are never forgotten?"

The Queen sang:

> *Over all the earth four things I find*
> *Which leave no mark or trace behind:*
> *The eagle soaring bold and free,*
> *The ship which sails the foaming sea.*
> *The snake as o'er the rock he slips,*
> *And a lover's kiss on maiden lips.*

The King said, "Off with your head, oh Queen, unless you can answer me this: Why is it that no man knows where to find the truth?"

The Queen sang:

> *When first on earth the truth was born*
> *She crept into a hunting-horn.*

The hunter came, the horn was blown,
And where truth went was never known.

Ruggero said, "Off with your head, oh Queen, unless you can answer me this: "Where is it always dark in the best lighted room?"

The Queen sang:

> *Though great and good you seem to be,*
> *You still spread evil as wide as can be.*
> *And you may find, in church or camp,*
> *It's always dark beneath the lamp.*

Then Ruggero said, "Off with your head, oh Queen, unless you can answer this question: What two things become light and white and bright, and fly upward as they perish?"

Then the Queen sang:

The Good man's soul, as he does die,
The breaking wave while darting high
Fly upward in a dash of white
And before they perish, live in light.

King Ruggero said, "What manner of woman you may be on earth I know not. Certainly I've never encountered your like before. God knows that we men would have scant share therein. Now off with your head, oh Queen, unless you can answer me this: I slew a man in battle, and yet I slew him not. How was that possible?"

The Queen sang:

From you his death did come, my lord,
Yet, not by you, but by your sword.
Such difference, as I have heard,
Is not in deed, but in the word.
However it came, the blood was spilt,
The deed was yours, and yours the guilt.
But if I beat you in riddles that you play,
You'll have caused your death and nothing to say.

King Ruggero looked as if he had received a hard blow, and many who were in the hall thought that he was beginning to feel less easy as to his riddling. However, he kept up his hope and declared: "Off with your head, oh Queen, unless you can answer me this: There were three on the

water, three under the water, and three flying in the air, and yet the nine were one?"

The Queen sang:

> *Three and three or thirty-three,*
> *However many there may be,*
> *In sunshine or in stormy weather*
> *Make but one flock, all together.*

Ruggero said, "I saw an eagle dart onward fast as an arrow, yet he did not use his wings; he held in his beak a fish, which he had never caught, and never seen. Off with your head, oh Queen, unless you can answer me that riddle."

So, the Queen sang:

> *The eagle on an ice-floe stood,*
> *Which floated headlong down the flood,*
> *That eagle held in beak or claws*
> *A ravenous pike, between whose jaws*
> *A fish was held, upon my word!*
> *Caught by the pike and not the bird.*
> *As you in the end will prove to be*
> *Caught by yourself and not by me;*
> *From your vein there came the bane*
> *With which you will at last be slain*

It seemed in that minute to King Ruggero that the room grew dark, and that he were a thousand miles away in a snow-cold, silent land, while a voice within pleaded with him to leave this strife of riddles and retire in time, and beg mercy

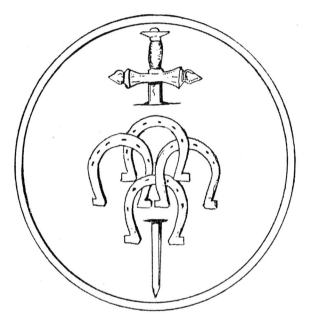

of the wonderful woman who laughed him to scorn. But
then his evil spirit rose within him and said, "There is no vic-
tory without danger. Go on! "So he roused himself, and
drank a mighty cup of wine and said, "Off with your head,
oh Queen, unless you can answer me this: There was a thing

trodden underfoot night and day by a sorry creature. It was cast out on a dunghill and given as a rare and costly thing to a king, who prized it highly. What was that thing?"

The Queen sang:

> *A sorry jade its horse-shoes wore,*
> *And when at last its life was over,*
> *While on the dunghill as it lay,*
> *There came a weapon-smith one day,*
> *Who took the shoes, and, as I've heard,*
> *From them he made a wondrous sword,*
> *So keen of edge, so apt to strike,*
> *No one had ever seen such like.*
> *Through all the realm its fame did ring,*
> *And so it came unto the king,*
> *Who ever wore it by his side,*
> *And oft its edge in battle tried.*
> *In all of which a lesson lies:*
> *When, true as steel, all men may rise,*
> *Even from vilest earthly things,*
> *To be the pride and joy of kings.*

This was so well sung that all present applauded, and King Ruggero said, "I did not know myself that there was such a good lesson in my riddle. But off with your head, Oh Queen, unless you can answer me this: A man once saw himself

where he had never been, but when he came into that place
he never saw himself again."

The Queen sang:

> *Looking in a river, he*
> *Did himself reflected see*
> *By himself he thus was seen,*
> *Where he truly never had been.*
> *Gazing there and looking round,*
> *In he fell, and so was drowned.*
> *So when there, it is very plain,*
> *He never saw himself again."*

The King paused at this as if it had caused in him deep thought, and then said, "Off with your head, oh Queen, unless you can answer me this: Who is the guide who will not show you the way unless he be carried?"

The Queen sang:

> *The lantern guides you in the dark,*
> *Wherever you go, the way to mark,*
> *And yet it will not aid a whit,*
> *Unless in hand you carry it.*
> *Little you know of the light*
> *Which guides me in this path aright.*

The King said, "Off with your head, oh Queen, unless you can answer me this: Who is he that when buried in a brown garment rises again as a giant, and has thousands of children, who cry aloud when they feel warm?"

The Queen sang:

> *To rise again, the chestnut, he*
> *In his brown coat must buried be,*
> *Then, giant-like, from every limb*
> *There fall a thousand like to him,*
> *And all of them, ere they expire,*
> *Burst with a crack when on the fire.*
> *So in this life of woes or joys*
> *Are many who never make a noise,*
> *Nor raise in honor any din*
> *Until they feel the heat within*
> *The fire on which ambition feeds*
> *Warms it up to glorious deeds.*

"Yea," said the King, "ambition, like the salamander, feeds on fire. But answer me this, oh Queen, if you do not want your head beheaded: What are the two beings, one of which flies away when it is hot, and settles down firmly where it is cold, while the other does the contrary?"

The Queen sang:

> *The wild bird dreads the wintertime,*
> *And flies unto a warmer clime,*

To sunny lands beyond the sea,
Even to Egypt it may be,
Where the grave storks in silence stray,
By ancient ruins far away,
And Norland swallows flit and play;
But water, when it feels the heat,

Makes up aloft a quick retreat,
Still soaring, bird-like, ever higher
The more it's kept upon the fire;
But when it's frozen, in a trice
It sinks to earth as heavy ice.

Such differences Nature wears,
So varied are the forms she bears.
Even so, we see the poet's soul,
Warmed by success, escape control,
High soaring in prosperity,
But frozen by adversity.
It's the same moral, on my word !
Drawn from a chestnut or a bird.

That, too, was well drawn out," said the King. "But, off with your head, oh Queen, if you cannot answer me this: Who are the five in one who are welcomed everywhere all over the world, who make their way freely to all lords and kings, who cause wars and weddings, great sin, and great joy?"

The Queen sang:

G and I and F and T,
Joined to S, five sisters be,
Since in language, it is said,
Every letter is a maid.
GIFTS, above all earthly things,
Make their way to lords and kings.

Gifts lend to war its carriage;
Gifts cause full many a marriage;
Gifts oft lead to greatest sin,
Yet with them much joy we win.

> *Get what we may by work or thrift,*
> *Nothing glads us like a gift.*

The King said, "Off with your head, oh Queen, unless you can answer me this: Who runs faster the more clothes he puts on, and the greater the burden he carries?"

The Queen sang:

> *The ship flies faster in the gale,*
> *The more it spreads or carries sail.*
> *Sails are its clothing, as we know.*
> *Without them it could never go.*
> *The faster it will sail the sea,*
> *However great the load may be.*
> *Its speed is in the clothes it wears,*
> *And in the burden which it bears.*

"Yea," said the King, "even so it seems to me that the more I heap my riddles on you the more eloquently you answer them. But, oh Queen, off with your head, unless you can answer me this: Who is the sorcerer who shows to every man who meets him his equal, however brave he may be, and to

every woman her match in beauty?"

The Queen sang:

> *In a mirror we behold*
> *Iron for iron, gold for gold.*
> *However fair we seem or see,*

Yet in that our equals be.
No special figure does it wear,
But every other's likeness bear,
As parrots give all voices known,
Yet have no language of their own.

Then the King said, "Off with your head, oh Queen, unless you can answer me this: Who gives more victuals to the world than all the charitable people in it put together, and wastes all her substance in so doing, yet who never yet got any thanks for it?"

The Queen sang:

> *By the oven all the meat,*
> *Or bread, is baked which mortals eat.*
> *Much wood for food does she require,*
> *So wastes her life in burning fire.*
> *We were indeed in sorry case*
> *Without the oven and her grace;*
> *But none are left in this our day*
> *Whoever to the oven pray,*
> *Or render thanks to fire in rhyme,*
> *As others did in the olden time.*

The King said, "Off with your head, oh Queen, unless you can answer me this: Who is the traveler who never rests on his journey, and yet finds time to enter every house?"

The Queen sang:

The golden sun, who shines on high,
Is ever travelling in the sky.
Never weary, never worn,
He tresses on to night from morn,
Yet he, while hurrying on his ways,

Through every door and window strays,
And lingers long in every home
Wherever he may chance to come;
Even as a king should show his face

> *Unto all men with gentle grace,*
> *That all may think with joy thereon,*
> *As if they had beheld the sun.*

The King said, "Off with your head, oh Queen, unless can answer me this: Who were the four who kissed, the four who wept, the four who embraced, when two lovers parted?"

The Queen sang:

> *Every time when two are parted,*
> *If the pair be tender-hearted,*
> *Their four eyes are weeping blindly,*
> *Their four lips are kissing kindly,*
> *And four arms with pressing faces,*
> *Giving rapturous embraces.*

The King said, "Off with your head, oh Queen, unless you can answer me this: Who are the two, one dead, and the other alive, who treat one another every time they drink wine, drop for drop, never gaining, never losing?"

The Queen sang:

With a toper and his glass
This must always come to pass.
He makes the glass with liquor swim.
The glass then gives it unto him.
Thus it is between them they
Give glass for glass the livelong day.

"Good that!" cried the King. "It just reminds me of something . . ." Here he drank a full goblet of red wine, and sighed soundly, and then said, "Off with your head, oh Queen, unless you can answer me this: Where are the horses which will never be ridden, the lights that can never be numbered, the webs which will never be woven by woman's hand, the pens which never write, the puddings which can never be eaten, the staff with which no man ever walks yet which many women bear, and the button which never held a garment?"

The Queen sang:

> *Sea-horses never by man were mounted,*
> *The stars in heaven never counted,*
> *Cobwebs for weaving are too light,*
> *With pig pens none can ever write*
> *Plum-pudding stones no man can eat.*
> *With distaffs men we never meet.*
> *Bachelor's buttons, bright as gold,*
> *Did never any garment hold.*

The King exclaimed, "Seven *at a* blow! But off with your head, oh Queen, unless you can answer me this: Who are the seven sisters who are in all things, and without whom nothing can be seen and nothing imagined?"

The Queen sang:

> *One or all of colors seven*
> *Are in all things under heaven;*

Nothing cones into our mind
In which we no color find,
For when all their flight have taken,
White or black must still remain.
So when the rainbow flies away
What then remains is night or day.

The King said, "Off with your head, oh Queen, unless you can answer this question: What is that which is nothing and void, yet which holds fast and firm?"

The Queen sang:

A button-hole is truly naught,
Yet, when it's by the button caught,
It holds a garment fast and tight,
If I have read your riddle right.

The King replied, "Off with your head, oh Queen, unless you can answer me this: What is the one animal from which every man has had food, drink, and clothing?"

The Queen sang:

> *That must be the ox, I think.*
> *From his horns do all men drink,*
> *Of his flesh do all men eat.*
> *And his leather clothes our feet.*

Ruggero said, "Off with your head, oh queen, unless you can answer me this: What was that thing which you have often seen, which first gave shelter, then food, then joy, and then light?"

The queen sang:

> *That was a shell, it seems to me,*
> *Which housed a creature in the sea.*
> *A man there came who ate it up,*
> *And used the shell as drinking-cup*
> *For ale or wine. Then, after all,*
> *It hung as lamp in a cattle-stall.*

Yet you yourself, Oh King, confess
Could never before this riddle guess?

Ruggero looked hard and grim, and then said, "It is true, for I never did yet understand what the *light* meant. If you

had turned it full on me, I would have lost my life. But unless you yourself are some evil spirit or witch, I know not how you could tell what I knew or did not know. But, off with your head, oh Queen, unless you can answer me this: Who is she who has no tongue, yet talks distinctly, repeats everything which is told to her, and yet is no gossip, and is the more admired the louder she cries?"

The Queen sang:

> *Echo has no tongue, but she*
> *Often talks so perfectly*
> *That the travelers who stray*
> *In lonely places far away,*
> *Amid ancient walls and caverned rocks,*
> *Full often deem her one who mocks.*
> *And in the silent twilight hour,*
> *When elfin creatures use their power,*
> *When they hear strange echoes ringing,*
> *Think they hear the fairies singing,*
> *Or when some loving nightingale*
> *Is singing sweetly in a vale,*
> *And the music to the plain*
> *Thus redoubled comes again —*
> *Then echo seems revealed to you*
> *In her sweetest mystery quite true*
> *All that she hears she tells again,*
> *And yet she is no gossip vain.*

And the clearer is her voice,
The more to hear it all rejoice ;
And she certainly is quite like me
Since I only answer truthfully.

"Hum! That is truth without fact," said Ruggero. "Now,

Queen, off with your head, unless you can answer me this: Who enters a room without going in, or goes in without entering, opens the door, yet is no porter or servant and has a beard in one country but in none other?"

The Queen sang:

> *The key which fits into the lock*
> *Goes further than the men who knock.*
> *It is on the edge of every hall,*
> *Yet hardly in the place at all.*
> *It was the door to you, oh King,*
> *And yet it is no living thing;*
> *And its wards in the German tongue*
> *Are called a beard' when said or sung.*

"Well!" exclaimed Ruggero. "If you are not a learned woman, you are certainly learning to be one, and will not miss the mark. Off with your head, oh Queen, unless you can answer me this: There are two sisters, who have a friend who is often in their company. The two are divided, yet firmly united. Whatever comes in their way they wound sore and cut in twain, but their friend heals the wounds."

The Queen sang:

> *Scissors are the sisters two,*
> *Who never part, whatever they do;*
> *Both united to one end,*

And the needle is their friend.
  However they may cut their foes,
  What they wound, the needle sews.

Ruggero said, "Off with your head, oh Queen, unless you

can answer me this: Who is the fierce thief who, armed with a poisoned dagger, steals only from the fairest what is sweetest, and is himself robbed of all that he steals, yet, robber though he be, there is not a church in the land to which he has not given candles?"

The Queen sang:

> *The fairest creatures are the flowers,*
> *And from them in summer hours*
> *The bee, that busy little thing,*
> *Armed with his poison sting,*
> *Steals their honey when he can,*
> *And is robbed in turn by man,*
> *Yet offers for the church's sake,*
> *The wax from which men tapers make.*
> *That as a lesson men may see*
> *The light which comes from industry.*

"A good lesson," said Ruggero. "But off with your head, oh Queen, unless you can answer me this: There are a hundred who have no beginning or end, and they are all in one, who is endless as they are. They are bound everyone to his

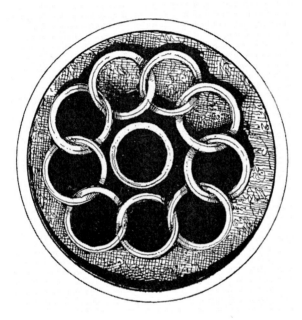

next, and when unbound and free they bind others for life."

The Queen sang:

> *Rings have no end, in them we see*
> *The emblem of eternity.*

When made of gold, all in a chain,
Still a circle it does remain.
And with but one, you will agree,
A loving pair may wedded be.

The King said, "Off with your head, oh Queen, unless you can answer me this: Who is that when he sinks down in his bed does great harm, but far more when he rises from it?'

The Queen sang:

> Dried in summer by the sun,
> Then the stream no more can run.
> With the water gone or low,
> Over it afoot we go.
> Much we miss its golden gleam,
> Much the cattle need their stream.
> Wagons pass where once the boat
> With its crew was wont to float,
> And the swallows chirp or nest
> Where the fishes used to rest.
> But it's worse in thawing Spring,
> When the crow on early wing
> Sees the floods, from ice set free,
> Rushing wildly to the sea.
> Then madly up the river leaps,
> As depths are added to his deeps,
> And, like a wolf before the hounds

In rage over all the country bounds.
Thus, if he rise or if he fall,
He brings great sorrow to us all.
So in life do all things go
What flies too high oft sinks too low.

> *Then pray to God, your destiny*
> *May never too unequal be.*

"Well sung and sermoned to a small text," said Ruggero. "But off with your head, oh Queen, unless you can answer me this: What goes from a tail to a head—yea, to royal Heads—and how does that which lived in disgrace confer honor?"

The Queen sang:

> *The ostrich in its tail may wear*
> *The splendid plume, so bright and fair,*
> *Which proudly waves wherever seen,*
> *In addition, gives a glory to a queen!*

The King said, "Off with your head, oh Queen, unless you can answer me this: "What is that which runs all day yet never stirs, which sings all the time yet never utters a word, and has the longest tail of any creature on earth?"

The Queen sang:

> *The spinning-wheel, which ever whirrs,*
> *And runs all day yet never stirs,*

115

And bears an endless tail of thread,
Is she of whom these things are said.

Then King Ruggero said, "Off with your head, oh Queen, unless you can answer me this: What is that which runs all

the time from one house to another, and from village to village by means of it all news is carried and yet is not gossip?"

The Queen sang:

A by-path runs over hill and dale.

On it is carried many a tale,
But for it, and it alone,
Scant news, I think, would ever be known.
By means of it all gossip's heard,
And yet it never speaks a word.

King Ruggero said, "Off with your head, oh Queen, unless you can answer me this: Who is it that who embraces my wife tightly and far oftener than I, yet of whom I am not jealous?"

The Queen sang:

> *Your queen's small waist is circled round,*
> *And by a golden girdle bound.*
> *He holds her fast the livelong day.*
> *With him she does in public play,*
> *And while awake, from first to last,*
> *The girdle always holds her fast.*

The King said, "Off with your head, oh Queen, unless you can answer me this: What are the only creatures which are truly attached to me and bound to me for life, who suit and adapt themselves to my ways, yet on whom I ever trample as in scorn?"

The Queen sang:

> *Your shoes do most exactly suit*
> *Themselves by use unto your foot;*
> *They too are bound to you by strings,*
> *As are no other earthly things;*

Despite their work nothing's required,
And yet you trample them in the mire.

The King said, "Off with your head, oh Queen, unless you can answer me this question: There was one who was buried alive, yet he rose again. Once more he was slain with a blade, yet would not die; again his inner being was beaten with rods out of his body, yet he lived. Then he was burned and boiled, yet after all he was stronger than ever, full of life, and giving life unto men."

The Queen sang:

> *The barley buried in the ground*
> *Grew up, and multiplied was found.*
> *Cut with a sickle, it's not dead,*
> *For still its soul is in its head;*
> *Thrashed with a flail, it does survive,*
> *And boiled and brewed, it's still alive,*
> *Though first as ale it shows its spirit,*
> *Such is its power and its merit.*

The King said, "Off with your head, oh Queen, unless you can answer me this: What holds even a king or a queen by the nose, yet gives them no offense?"

The Queen sang:

121

When the roses are in bloom,
Their rapturing perfume
Holds you by the nose, and yet,
You are not annoyed by it.

The King said, "Off with your head, oh Queen, unless you can answer me this: What is that which is deprived of its eyes that we may see?"

The Queen sang:

That is the mask which hides your face,
And covers it in every place,
All save the eyes, which cannot be,
For had it eyes you would not see.

Ruggero said, "Off with your head, oh Queen, unless you can answer this question: Who are the poorest men in the world, yet who always lay on gold?"

The Queen sang:

In the pictures artists paint
Many an image of a saint,
Poor indeed, yet always found
In a shining golden ground.

The King said, "Off with your head, oh Queen, unless you can answer me this: Who is the true companion who always comes in dire need stark naked to aid his master?"

The Queen sang:

In hour of need the bravest lord
Is always aided by his sword.
Leather, wood, or iron he wears,
And often a golden helmet bears,
But his coat is stripped away
When he comes bare into the fray.

The King said, "Off with your head, oh Queen, unless you can answer me this question: Who are the thousands of serpents which draw their life from us, yet whom we cherish with care?"

The Queen sang:

Hairs which grow on every head
Black or golden, brown or red,
When into the water thrown,
Change to serpents, as is known.
Yet, we all, with constant care,
Guard these serpents, which we wear.

The King said, "Off with your head, oh Queen, unless you can answer me this: What is that which is clothing for many yet nakedness for others?"

The Queen sang:

> *Near is my shift, more near my skin,*
> *On me it's but a garment thin,*
> *With it alone in dire distress,*
> *We are in utter nakedness,*

But on the bear his skin and hair
Make heavy clothes for him to wear.

Ruggero said, "Off with your head, oh Queen, unless you

can answer me this: Who was the thief who stole from me a white coat for which he repaid me with a grey one?"

The Queen sang:

> *By night, when all are sound asleep,*
> *A grey wolf came and stole your sheep,*
> *Whose good white skin, as I do ween,*
> *Had else your winter garment been.*
> *That wolf you did pursue and slay,*
> *And took from him his garment grey.*

Ruggero said, "Off with your head, oh Queen, unless you can answer me this: Who is the knave who often holds us by the throat with strong grip, nor lets us go until we give him somewhat?"

The Queen sang:

> *Of all the knaves that be, the worst,*
> *Who often comes to us is Thirst.*
> *He holds us by the throat, I think,*
> *Nor goes until we give him drink.*

"Aye, that is true," remarked Ruggero, "and he holds me even now. Page, bring me a can of ale! But off with your head, oh Queen, unless you can answer me this: How was a kingdom given away by the help of a goose, a sheep, and a bee?"

The Queen sang:

> *From the goose there came the quill*
> *Which made the pen, which wrote the will.*

> *The sheep then yielded up his skin,*
> *Which provided parchment thin.*
> *And from the bee they next did steal*
> *The wax with which they made a seal.*
> *Well, you surely know without the three*
> *No conveyances at all could be.*

Ruggero replied, "Off with your head, oh Queen, unless you can answer me this: What is that which loses its name when it falls, and takes it again when it gets up, and runs on?"

The Queen sang:

> *The stream, which leaps a precipice*
> *While jumping into the abyss,*
> *just then, by other name we call,*
> *For it becomes a Waterfall.*
> *But when it onwards runs, the same,*
> *Again resumes its former name.*

The King said, "Off with your head, oh Queen, unless you can answer me this: Which bird has above all others has the highest note?"

The Queen sang:

> *The lark, who, when the morning breaks,*
> *His flight over all to heaven takes*
> *And singing onward, high and far,*

Salutes the parting silver star
Even before the rising sun
His golden course has well begun
Since all are far below his call,
I deem the highest of them all.

The King grumbled, "Off with your head, oh Queen, unless you can answer me this: What is the eye which sees no one yet which all delight to see."

The Queen sang:

The flower which we the Day's Eye call,
Known as the Daisy unto all,
When, dimmed with one fair drop of dew,
Seems sweetly turned with love to you.
Therefore, with love that eye we see,
Although it ever blind may be.

The King declared, "Off with your head, oh Queen, unless you can answer me this: What is like the two clearest things on earth yet far beyond them?"

The Queen sang:

> *The diamond is like ice and glass,*
> *And often might for either pass,*
> *Yet like a gent of noble birth*
> *It far surpasses both in worth.*
> *Even so, a noble heart we prize*
> *Over men who're like him in our eyes.*
> *True faith all things does go beyond,*
> *And is the spirit diamond.*

The King said, "Off with your head, oh Queen, unless you can answer me this: What race is it that is always in the world, yet which never has children?"

The Queen sang:

> *Of animals the mule alone*
> *Has never offspring of his own.*
> *Like men of noble sires begot,*
> *Whose lives, however, end in naught.*

The King responded, "Off with your head, oh Queen, unless you can answer me this: I truly saw seven birds hatched from one egg. How was that possible?"

The Queen sang:

A sailor from beyond the sea
Once brought an ostrich egg for you to see
As in your hall the shell did rest,
A starling came and made his nest,
And from that curious shelter sprung
In time full seven of his young.

The King then said, "Off with your head. Oh Queen, unless you can answer me this: What is that whitest brightest thing which yet leaves black marks and what the very blackest which when used becomes white?"

The Queen sang:

Silver's white, and yet, alack!
Draws on parchment lines so black
While the charcoal, black as night,
Burns to ashes which are white.
Those who are fairest to our eyes

143

Too often deal in darkest lies,
While others who are grim to view,
Still utter naught which is not true.

The King said, "Off with your head, oh Queen, unless you can answer this: There was a man who sailed far over the sea, then dwelt in a home on the shore, and when he died was buried in a great coffin, yet he always slept in the same building, and he is still in it."

The Queen sang:

He who sailed the ocean more,
Drew his ship up on the shore,
Rarely left it for a minute,
And when dead was buried in it.

The King said, "Off with your head, oh Queen, unless you can answer me this: There was an oak tree, it became an apple tree, and by it there stood a house which no man ever entered."

The Queen sang:

On an oaken panel fair,
A house was carved and standing there,
Beside it rose an apple tree,
Thus it came to pass, I see!

145

The King said, "Off with your head, oh Queen, unless you answer me this: Who is cradled in a snow-white coffin yet never buried?"

The Queen sang:

The bird or fowl, whatever it be,
Born in a snow-white egg we see,
Which coffin-like cloth holds them well
Until it's time to peck the shell.
And when their life has reached its spin
They're eaten up by beast or man.

147

The King said, "Off with your head, oh Queen, unless you can answer me this: Who is the grim and fierce watchman who slays and devours thieves, who dread him more than any one on earth, yet is dearly loved by every little child, who fears him not?"

The Queen sang:

> *It's the Cat, who in a house*
> *Slays and eats both rat and mouse.*
> *But though to them so fierce and wild,*
> *He's loved by every little child.*
> *Thus to kings I'd have it come,*
> *Feared abroad, yet loved at home.*

The King said, "Off with your head, oh Queen, unless you can answer me this: "Who is it whose name is a byword for folly yet by whom all wisdom is made known unto man?"

The Queen sang:

> *The squalling goose, with flapping wing,*
> *Is always called a foolish thing.*
> *A blundering bird, of little wit,*
> *Yet with its quills, all books are writ.*
> *For every word of wisdom still*
> *Is written with the grey goose quill.*

The King said, "Off with your head, oh Queen, unless you can answer me this: What is that one thing entirely dead, and which never grew, yet which hides itself in winter and spring and is seen during the summer and autumn?"

The Queen sang:

The grey rock standing in a river,
Which had been there and dead forever
When the torrents rushing rise,
Then is hidden from our eyes.
But when the summer heat has dried,
The water up, it can soon be spied.
It never had life, it never grew,
Yet boldly rises then to view.
Even as it is with so many men
Whom we rarely see, save when
The sunlight of prosperity
About us shines. Oh, then we see
Them plainly, but they're lost again
When misery comes like winter rain.

King Ruggero said, "Off with your head, oh Queen, unless you can answer me this: What is born in its coffin, which dies if taken from it, and cannot rise again unless it be buried in that coffin?"

The Queen sang:

The nut which in a shell we see

Does seem confined to me.
If once that coffin we should open,
The nut will die beyond all hope.
But buried deeply in the plain,
It rises into life again.

King Ruggero said, "What is that hard mother who, wedded to a harder mate, produces a still harder son? Answer or I'll have your head!"

The Queen sang:

Lead is hard, I well admit,
Copper harder, far from it
But the two together melted,
In the fiery furnace smelted,
Make of bronze a glowing ball

> *Which is hardest of them all,*
> *Out of which the smith with might*
> *Shapes the sword with which you fight.*

King Ruggero said, "Off with your head, oh Queen, unless you can answer me this: What is that serpent, which coiled around a tree, that often gives to man food and drink which is forbidden to many?"

The Queen sang:

> *The Vine, as every one may see,*
> *Coils serpent-like around a tree,*
> *Giving to many grades for food,*
> *And wine fermented from their blood,*
> *That drink forbidden to the churl,*
> *Which is the joy of prince or earl.*

King Ruggero said, "Off with your head, oh Queen, unless you can answer me this: Where are the people so cruel that they cannot dance with joy unless some one is beaten and cries."

The Queen sang:

Where the tambourine they beat
Maidens dance with fluttering feet,
To the merry drum they bound,
Which, till it's beaten, gives no sound,

And in many things, I know,
Many men let themselves go.

King Ruggero said, "Off with your head, oh Queen, unless
you can answer me this: Who is the thief who often carries

away clothing, yea, and many other things, yet never took them home, never used them, and never sold them?"

The Queen sang:

> *When the linen's hung to dry,*
> *And the Wind is roaring high,*
> *Often he steals maid or man*
> *All the clothing that he can,*
> *Whirls it merrily on high*
> *To some field, then lets it ly,*
> *Or, as in an elfin joke,*
> *Leaves it swinging on an oak.*
> *Out the angry housewife flies,*
> *And to catch the runner tries,*
> *Sees her petticoat one minute*
> *Dance as if an elf were in it,*
> *Then her husband's linen breeches*
> *Capering as with the witches,*
> *While shifts fly off with flapping hem,*
> *As if a goblin were in them.*
> *These, as we do often find,*
> *Are the robberies of the Wind,*

Yet though it makes all things fly, it
Never gains a penny by it.

The King said, "Off with your head, oh Queen, unless you
can answer this: When and where did pigs fly through the

air with their tails upwards?"

The Queen sang:

> *There was a castle sore beset,*
> *And little food its men could get;*
> *They had among their friends without*
> *One like a giant, strong and stout,*
> *It chanced one day while lurking near,*
> *He saw a drove of swine appear.*
> *No one was nigh. As quick as thought*
> *He one by one the swine up-caught,*
> *In addition, light as urchins throw their balls,*
> *He hurled them over the castle walls.*
> *The men besieged were gay as gigs*
> *To see this joyous rain of pigs.*
> *It was a wondrous sight to see*
> *How the pigs flew so gloriously!*
> *Tails up, they hustled through the air,*
> *Until not a single swine was there.*
> *'Thus it was he served his liege,*
> *Thus, it was he broke the siege.*
> *Even so, often to operate it befalls,*

When sin assails our spirit's walls,
Some blessed angel, prompt and kind,
Throws pious thoughts into our mind,
And we, even in our worst distress,
Are turned to truth and righteousness.

"By my faith, this is a good tale and well moralized!" Ruggero declared. "Now, off with your head, oh Queen, unless you can answer me this: What is ever rising, ever going up on a mountain side, yet which never gets nearer to the top?"

The Queen sang:

> *A tree upon the mountain side*
> *Grows high and spreads its branches wide:*
> *Thus certainly, before our eyes,*
> *Upon the mount the tree does rise,*
> *Perhaps upon a height sublime,*
> *Still going upward all the time;*
> *But though it grow, or if it stop,*
> *It's never nearer to the top.*
> *Thus many grow, yet all in vain,*
> *For what they seek, they never attain.*

"Aye," said the King, "I wonder whether I am really nearer to the top of this hill of riddles than I was when I began. But now, oh Queen, off with your head, unless you can answer me this: What was made only to fly in the air, yet which has no wings?"

The Queen sang:

> *The leather ball is only made*
> *To fly as birds fly, when it is played.*
> *Yet, it has neither beak nor wings,*

Nor is it like to flying things.
And, having made its flight or bound,
It falls straightway to the ground.
Even as men of little wit
Try that for which they are unfit,

And after flight and effort sore,
Fall back unto the earth once more.

The King said, "Off with your head, oh Queen, unless you can answer me this: What are the horned cattle which climb trees and walls, where no goat could go, yet which are without feet?"

The Queen sang:

Without a foot, without a tail,
And yet with horns we see the snail,
Browsing and rocking at its ease,
Upon the tops of lofty trees.
For well we know that sure and slow
Does often to the highest go.

Then said King Ruggero, "Riddles ninety-and-nine have I asked you on your life or mine, and I truly mean that should you lose, you and your family shall die. Now we have come to the last, and as death for one of us stands but a few moments off, I would like to know by what art you have answered, so promptly, riddles over which the shrewdest man living would

166

have had to take much time? And for my last question: Off
with your head, oh Queen, unless you can answer me this:
What was it that my mother, when dying, when no one was
near, told me in secret, which secret I have guarded all my life?"

The Queen said:

*When your mother died, there was another present invisibly, and that
was I. She told you to beware of the fairy Bellaria, who, unless you refrained
from cruel war and oppression, would be your bane and death. Well, I
am Bellaria, who was made Queen for your punishment. And as to
answering your riddles, Oh weak and wicked King, know that I read
them every one of them in your mind before they were uttered.*

Then the King rose in mad rage, and drew his sword, and
struck at the Queen-fairy to slay her. But a dizziness seized
him. He dropped his sword, which went to the ground hilt
downward, and he fell upon the point, which passed through
his heart. Then there was a great outcry in the hall, and
many servants tried to raise the King, but he was dead. And
in the tumult the fairy Bellaria vanished. Nor was she ever
seen again after that, though it is commonly believed that
she often appeared to her husband and her son. And this son

grew up into a man of great strength and wonderful wisdom, who in after days became King over all that land.

Thus were the hundred riddles made
Which in this book you now have read.
Many may deem them trifling things,
Yet practice in them ever brings
Great quickness to the youthful mind,
As all may soon by trial find.
Those who soon trace a riddle out
Are quick at solving any doubt;
And many a thing is taught in schools
Not half so good for curing fools
As Riddling is. The thing is true,
men of yore far better knew.

FINIS

Charles Godfrey Leland (1824–1903) was an American humorist, writer, and folklorist. Primarily known during his lifetime for his comic *Hans Breitmann's Ballads* (1871), he wrote extensively on folklore, paganism, and linguistics. He is author of *Pidgin-English Sing-Song* and *Aradia, or the Gospel of the Witches*.

Jack Zipes is professor emeritus in the Department of German, Scandinavian, and Dutch at the University of Minnesota. He is author of more than forty books, including *Tales of Wonder: Retelling Fairy Tales through Picture Postcards* and *Fearless Ivan and His Faithful Horse Double-Hump*, both from the University of Minnesota Press.